THE
WHINGDINGDILLY

THE
WHINGDINGDILLY

written and illustrated by BILL PEET

HOUGHTON MIFFLIN COMPANY BOSTON

In memory of a wonderful dog

Scamp flopped down heavily on the porch with a mournful sigh. The old farm dog had been in a miserable mood for weeks and no one knew why. Not even his best friend Orvie Jarvis could guess what the trouble might be.

Before the dark mood crept over him Scamp had been a happy carefree dog. He was always up early racing out to the barn lot ahead of Orvie, eager for the boy to finish the morning chores so the two of them could go rambling around the countryside.

Now Scamp moped on the porch until Orvie called him. Then he came drooping along at the boy's heels, sad-eyed and listless, not caring how long it took to finish the chores.

"What's come over you, ole Scamp?" asked Orvie one day. "What makes you so sad?"

Scamp's only reply was a dreary sigh. There was no way of telling Orvie that he was tired of being a dog. That he wanted to be a horse. Not just any horse. Scamp wanted to be a great horse like Palomar the giant Percheron who lived on the farm just across the road.

Back in those days there were lots of buggies and wagons so horses were very important. Palomar was especially important. He had won blue ribbons at horse shows and fairs all over the country so he was famous.

People traveled hundreds of miles just for a look at the great horse. And Palomar always treated the crowd to a good show by high-stepping around and around his pasture in true champion style. Everyone admired Palomar, but no one ever gave Scamp so much as a glance. No one but his friend Orvie.

Scamp often dreamed that he was the famous Palomar surrounded by an admiring crowd. Sometimes when the dog was sure no one was watching he would imitate the great horse and go high-stepping around the barn lot with his nose in the air.

Then one day Orvie caught him at it.

"Ho! Ho! Scamp," he chortled. "What are you up to? Who do you think you are, you silly ole dog?"

Scamp had never felt so foolish in all his life. To be called a "silly ole dog" was more than he could bear. And while Orvie was busy feeding the chickens Scamp went slinking out of the barn lot and on down the road. He was running away.

Just where he was going he had no idea. But after trotting along for about a mile the dog found himself panting. It was a hot summer afternoon, much too hot to be trotting about in a shaggy fur coat, and when he came to a dense woods he stopped. Scamp had heard about this place. People believed that a wicked little witch lived there who possessed great magic power, and if anyone dared to enter the woods she might turn them to stone or into a toad.

But Scamp was in no mood to worry about a little witch, so in he went.
It was much cooler in the dark spooky woods and ever so quiet. The only
sound was the burbling of a brook running along through a jumble of rocks.

The brook finally trickled down to a crystal-clear pool where Scamp stopped to stare at his gloomy reflection. This was the first time he had taken a good look at himself, and more than ever he wished he were a horse. All at once the hair at the back of his neck bristled. Someone was watching. Quickly Scamp wheeled around looking right and left and then finally up into a sycamore. And there was the little witch leaning out the window of her tree house!

Scamp was on his feet all ready to run when the witch said, "So you want to be a horse do you?" And before you could say "scat!" she flew out the door and down the steps and was nose to nose with the bewildered dog.

"Why old Zildy can turn you into a horse in a twinkling," she said, patting him gently on the head. "Oh, but I can do much better than that, doggy. How would you like to be something fantastic? The only one of its kind in all the world? A marvelous magnificent something I call a whingdingdilly? What do you say?"

Scamp cocked his head in thought for a few seconds, then with a wag of the tail barked his "yes" bark.

"Good dog! So we'll get on with it!" she cried, snapping a twig off the sycamore. "I don't really need a wand. Any old thing will do. My magic power is all in the words. Just watch."

Suddenly Zildy was dancing about like a grasshopper, waving the twig in the air, and in her high screechy voice she recited the magic words.

"Diggety dawgety ziddle dee zump,
    We'll start right off with a camel hump.

Then camel hind legs skaroodle dee doo
With zebra stripes and a zebra tail too.

Now for a neck ker-snickety snaff
With squarish brown spots just like a giraffe.

Ka lumpity mumbo jumbo ka jellaphant,
Here's the big feet and front legs of an elephant.

Zum zum zaroot most anything goes,
So how about a rhinoceros nose.
Then elephant ears ker-flippety flop
And reindeer horns zilly-zop! Out the top."

"I've done it! I've done it!" Zildy cried gleefully. "There you are, dog.
The one and only whingdingdilly. Go take a look at yourself."

The sudden change had made him dizzy and Scamp tottered unsteadily on his new set of legs as he turned around to face the pool. What he saw was much too much to take in all at once, and with a loud rhino snort he went staggering backwards.

"See what I mean?" said the little witch. "You're one whopping big surprise. Now I'd better skeedaddle if I'm going to make cookies today." And Zildy scurried up the steps into the tree house leaving the whingdingdilly wondering what he would do.

Finally he decided he'd better go home. Just as he started off the witch called out the window, "Take care you don't step in my tulip bed with those big clumsy feet of yours!"

In the shadows of the sycamore were rows of bright yellow flowers and as he headed back through the trees he was careful to step around them.

Making his way through the dense woods had been easy for the dog, but now it was almost impossible for the whingdingdilly. It was a struggle every step of the way with his antlers catching on tree limbs, the rhino horns hooking onto vines, the clumsy elephant feet stumbling over logs and the camel feet tripping over the elephant feet. The going was so slow that it was near sundown when he finally made it to the edge of the woods.

As Scamp poked his head out through the trees he surprised a sow and her six piglets. Squealing in terror they went racing pell-mell away through the weeds.

"What a fright I must be," thought Scamp. "I'm in no shape to be running around in plain sight. No telling what people might do."

Then, stretching his long giraffe neck, he raised his head for a view of the countryside. As far as he could see the fields were deserted and so were the roads. All the farmers had gone to dinner, so there was a good chance of getting home without being seen.

As he lumbered out into the open road he found the going much easier. It was just a matter of keeping the long-striding camel legs from overrunning the plodding elephant legs. And he was clumping along at a pretty good clip when all at once he heard Orvie calling.

"Here Scamp! Here Scamp! Here Scamper boy!" He was coming up the road just over the next hill.

If Orvie should come face to face with a whingdingdilly, especially in the eerie light of evening, it might scare his scrawny little friend out of a year's growth. That wouldn't do.

In one clumsy leap Scamp was over a fence and went sprawling headlong into a wheatfield. There he remained flat to the ground scarcely breathing and as still as a wheat shock.

When Orvie came to the top of the hill he stopped for one last call, such a long loud "Here Scamper!" that it echoed for a mile across the countryside.

Then he listened for an answering bark. But there was only the faraway crowing of a rooster.

"Where could he be?" wondered Orvie as he turned and headed back down the road.

Scamp raised his head to watch until the boy was no more than a speck in the distance. Then with an effort he hauled himself to his feet and hobbled over the fence back onto the road.

By this time he was getting leg-weary and he went plodding along ever so slowly; it was growing dark when he finally reached the Jarvis farm.

Cautiously he pushed open the gate, tiptoed across the yard to the house and peeked in the kitchen window.

The family had just finished dinner. Everyone but Orvie, who sat at the table staring at his plate.

"Scamp is always home at dinnertime," said the boy. "Something's happened to him or he'd be here."

"If old Scamp's really gone for good," said his father, "then I'll tell you what. Armstrongs have a new colt and if they'll sell him he's all yours. How would you like that, son?"

"It's not the same," said Orvie. "You can't get to know a horse. Not like you can a dog. Ole Scamp understood just about everything I said. He was a lot smarter than any horse, and besides that he was a real friend."

Scamp could hardly believe his big flappy ears. So Orvie didn't really mean it when he called him a "silly ole dog." In fact Orvie thought he was smart, and Scamp heaved a great sigh of relief. But what would Orvie think of a whingdingdilly?

Scamp decided to wait until morning to find out, and he stood there in the dark until he was sure everyone had gone to bed. Then the whingding-dilly stretched out full length on the front porch with a monstrous yawn.

"Maybe this is nothing but a bad dream," he thought, "and when I wake up I'll be the same as ever." Pretty soon he was sound asleep and snoring just like a rhinoceros.

The next thing Scamp knew it was morning and Orvie was shouting, "Dad! Mom! Come quick! There's a thing! A-a great big thing out here!"

The whingdingdilly struggled to his feet looking wildly about for the big thing. Then suddenly he remembered that *he* was the thing and went stumbling backwards off the porch out into the yard. And in one clumsy leap he was over the fence and galloping away down the road.

His head was in such a whirl he didn't see the man driving his cows to pasture until he was almost upon them. In a panic the man jumped into a ditch and the bawling terrified cows went crashing through a fence scattering in all directions. Another man was so shocked at the sight of the gigantic beast he lost control of his tractor and the machine went plowing through a haystack to end up in a duck pond.

Then there was a near head-on collision with a horse and buggy. The horrified horse left the road in one leap to go scrambling up a telegraph pole buggy and all. Now the whingdingdilly didn't dare stop or even slow down and he kept going full gallop all the way back to the woods.

Scamp was hoping Zildy would understand his awful predicament and undo her magic spell. Once again he fought his way through the tangle of trees. When he reached the tree house he gave the door a resounding "thump" with his snout, then watched for Zildy to pop her head out the window. But no Zildy appeared. The shutters were latched and the door was locked and bolted.

"If she's gone," Scamp reasoned, "she'll be back sooner or later. So all I can do is wait."

It would be a long wait. Early that morning Zildy had packed her suitcase, spruced herself up in her fancy best and left on a trip to visit her sister in Massachusetts. She hadn't sailed away on a broomstick like most witches do. Zildy was in no hurry so she had taken the train. Now she was riding along in comfort munching on sugar cookies with no thought whatever of what might have happened to the whingdingdilly.

In the meantime all the farmers in the neighborhood had formed a small army, and with guns and pitchforks they followed the trail of huge footprints straight to the woods. But they didn't dare go in for now the woods were more frightening than ever.

"We'll wait him out," said big Moose Mulford, the leader of the army. "The minute the monster shows his face Powie! we'll pop 'im off."

The farmers stood watch on into the evening, then all through the night; and when morning came there was still no sign of the monster.

"From now on," yawned Moose, "we'll split up in bunches with some takin' the night watch and the others takin' the day."

But after watching the woods night and day for a week the biggest thing to come out was a rabbit. By this time news of the monster had spread all over the county, all the way to Central City, and finally to Claxton J. Pringle, the great showman.

C. J. Pringle's Palace of Living Wonders towered majestically above the city square. Over the main entrance was a sign reading, MENAGERIE OF THE MARVELOUS AND THE AMAZING. THE MOST COLOSSAL COLLECTION OF INCREDIBLE CREATURES TO BE SEEN ANYWHERE ON EARTH.

The great showman had traveled all over the world in search of spectacular new attractions for his menagerie, and when he read in the newspaper that a fantastic giant of a beast was running loose in the county, C.J. was jubilant.

"Eureka!" he cried. "Why if this beast is half what they say it is it could be worth a fortune. But first I must get my hands on the thing."

Within half an hour C.J. had rounded up his roughest toughest crew of roustabouts and they took off in their Hupperson autobus followed by a ten ton beast-moving van. The great showman was in a desperate hurry, so he went at top speed all the way with the horn blaring full blast warning everyone to clear the road.

And in no time they came skidding to a stop alongside the woods where all the farmers rushed out to greet them.

"If you've come after the monster," said Moose Mulford, "he's some-
where back in those trees. But you'd better be careful. He's a real whopper."

"The bigger the better," said C.J. Then turning to his men he warned,
"Don't get too rough. I want the beast all in one piece."

"Easy does it," they promised and with lassoes, chains and leg-irons the
roustabouts went charging into the woods.

By the time Scamp had discovered what all the crashing around in the brush was about he was surrounded. He tried to run, but after one turn around the sycamore the men closed in, grabbing onto his legs, his neck, and his tail.

46

In a fast and furious struggle they wrestled him to the ground, roped and chained him from head to foot, then dragged him away through the woods.

"Thunderation!" roared C.J. at first sight of the giant beast. "He is a whopper! No wonder there was such a big hullabaloo. Say now," he exclaimed, "there's a good name for the thing. A Hullabalooper! The Super Duper Hullabalooper."

"Suits him to a T," chuckled Moose Mulford. Now that the danger was past the farmers were a happy bunch. They were laughing and joking while the beast was being loaded into the van, and as C. J. Pringle and his crew headed back up the road toward the city the farmers gave them a rousing cheer.

That night the bewildered and bedraggled Super Duper Hullabalooper was hustled down a ramp into the basement of Pringle's Palace and left in a cage with other Living Wonders of the World.

There he remained while C.J. went bustling about the city getting placards printed and posters painted to advertise his fabulous new attraction: THE MOST COLOSSAL, THE MOST STUPENDOUS AND PHENOMENAL CREATURE IN ALL THE UNIVERSE! *Don't miss the Grand Presentation at C. J. Pringle's Palace of Living Wonders on the Great Day of July Twentieth!*

When the great day arrived Pringle's Palace was jammed to overflowing, with thousands more waiting in line outside.

"Keep calm everyone!" bellowed C.J. as the noisy excited crowd kept pushing and shoving for a closer look at the amazing beast high up on a pedestal. The Super Duper Hullabalooper was too much to believe. Some people poked at him with canes while others yanked on his tail to make sure the beast was real.

Now Scamp was even more famous than the great Palomar, and yet he had never been so miserable in all his life. He wished there was some way to escape, but he was always kept chained to the pedestal and after the show he was caged in the basement for the night. So it seemed that Scamp was doomed to spend the rest of his days as the greatest of all Living Wonders at Pringle's Palace.

Then one afternoon Zildy returned home. "Zarks!" she cried when she reached her tree house, "somebody's trampled my tulips, and I know who!"

All around the sycamore were the telltale elephant tracks and the camel tracks of the whingdingdilly.

"I'll get even," she muttered, "and don't worry whingdingdilly, I'll find you." Then Zildy shut her eyes to concentrate. "Now let me see. Let me see. M-m-m-m! Aha! So there you are! Living in a palace! A high falootin' somebody! A celebrity are you?!! Well I'll fix that!"

In one hop Zildy was up on a stump. Then aiming her umbrella in the exact direction of Central City the angry little witch exploded, "Whammy Ka Zammy Skrumbo Skaroof! Zigga Zum Zap! Zaroota Ker-Poof!"

And in one great purple "POOF!" the Super Duper Hullabalooper was gone. In its place stood a plain ordinary frowsy brown dog. The crowd was so flabbergasted that for a full minute they were left gaping in amazement. Then all at once they burst into an uproar of shouting, "It's a fake! It's a fake! The Hullabalooper is a hoax! We've been hornswoggled! We've been rooked! Claxton J. Pringle is a swindler and a crook!"

For the very first time the great showman was caught speechless. In a huffing puffing fury he seized the dog by the tail and the scruff of the neck, then hustled him off through the crowd.

"Out! Out! Out! and the devil take you!" he bellowed as he flung the dog out the front door.

In one bounce Scamp was on his feet racing down the street dodging in and out through the traffic. Now that he was free there was nothing more to worry about. Finding his way out of the big city was easy to do.

Dogs have a fine sense of direction and by nightfall Scamp was loping along a dusty road far out in the country.

"I'm lucky to be a dog," he said to himself, "with sense enough to find my way home. Even a great horse like Palomar might get lost in the big city."

Scamp had not felt so happy and carefree in a long time, and when he came over the last hill and spied the Jarvis house he barked joyfully.

Then as he came bounding into the yard Orvie leaped off the porch shouting, "Scamp! Scamp! It's ole Scamper! Scamp's come home!"

In a wild rough and tumble greeting the boy and the dog went sprawling in the grass.

"Scamp! You old rascal!" cried Orvie. "Where have you been?! Where have you been all this time?!"

"Rowf! Rowf!" replied Scamp which was as much as the dog could tell him. And of course Orvie would never guess where Scamp had been. Not in a zillion years.

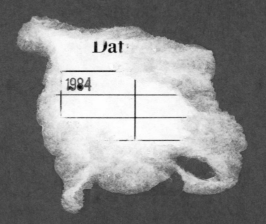